LULU AND THE SHAPE-SHIFTING HEALERS

THE FORGETTEN REALM
BOOK ONE

RHEA IRIS RIVERS &

OUR FORGOTTEN ALLIES

While the author strongly believes in the benefits of homeopathy and medicinal herbal treatments, readers are strongly urged to conduct their own research on each preparation. The information in this book is given in good faith. It is not intended to diagnose any physical or mental condition nor to serve as a substitute for informed medical advice or care. Please get in touch with your health professional for medical advice and treatment. Neither author nor the publisher can be held liable by any person for any loss or damage whatsoever which may arise from the use of this book or any of the information therein.

Edited by Michael Belvins, Omkari Kloostra

Illustrations by Rhea Rivers and Abode Firefly

Original Music, Into the Light, by Rhea Rivers

Sheet Music by Nic Leo

ISBN# 979-8-9909765-1-1 ebook / 979-8-9909765-2-8 print

Books:

Coloring Book -Lulu and the Shape-Shifting Healers (2024)

Lulu and the Shape-Shifting Healers— Volume I

The Forgotten Realm

Our Forgotten Allies, What's Your Frequency (2018)

CONTENTS

CHAPTER 1
WHO GOES THERE?

Our adventure begins from the back door. One crisp morning, as Lulu stepped outside her home, she noticed unusual footprints in her beautiful, enchanted garden. This garden, stunning and brimming with various colored flowers and lush green branches, was a sight to behold. These peculiar footprints were tiny in some places and more prominent in other areas within the garden, each uniquely different. Lulu's curiosity sparked, and she wondered what kind of creature could leave such an imprint on the ground.

Lulu left her home again the following day only to notice these odd footprints. But this time, something was different. The prints led up to her back door, traveled down the side of her home, ascended over the chimney, and disappeared over the peak of the roof. "What kind of creature could leave these peculiar little prints? Who goes there?" She said to herself. "It is time to meet my new neighbor, but how could I ever uncover the identity of this mysterious visitor?"

Then she considered how she might catch a glimpse

and perhaps a meeting. As night fell, Lulu left the warmth of her home and stepped into her enchanted garden. It was springtime, her favorite time of the year, and her garden was alive with blooming flowers and lush greenery. She felt right at home as she held her book on the magical properties of medicinal plants. Though still a student, she realized she had much to learn about the power each herb held. She carried a cozy, warm blanket and flashlight. Lulu felt the excitement about catching a glimpse of the peculiar new neighbor.

She found her secret spot in the garden, under the protection of the old Elder Tree, and nestled silently under the warmth of her blanket. Her blanket lay over the soft moss and grasses, covering many of the roots of this ancient tree. Using caution around the delicate nature of her injured knee, Lulu removed the support wrap to enjoy the outdoor air. Overhead, a beaming, pink full moon illuminated the night. The moon's glittering glow bathed the garden in a magical light and began to stir deep emotions. The pink moon is known to foster deeper connections- with a love partner, a friend, or a family member. As Lulu pondered this, she realized how she longed for deeper connections. She recalled the harrowing accident that left her unable to drive comfortably again and diminished her confidence in her abilities as a young, aspiring healer. The loss of her mother a year earlier had left an emptiness within her, and her father had never been a part of her life since her birth. She found happiness again when she enrolled in The School of Healing Arts after her high school graduation. The anticipation of possibly meeting her mysterious visitor filled her with a sense of wonder and hope.

Lulu in her Enchanted Garden

As Lulu lay there in her garden, she inhaled deeply, savoring the aroma of the night-blooming jasmine. In the distance, a cricket chirped. A soft, warm breeze caressed her skin. Before long, she couldn't help but drift off to sleep. She awoke to a cheerful song from her friend Bonkers, the blue-jay. Bonkers often visited her enchanted garden and loved singing to her whenever she was nearby. Disappointed not to have met her new neighbor, she left her enchanted, serene garden and returned home. As she walked up the steps to her back door, the adorable little peculiar footsteps appeared again. But this time, the footprints didn't stop at the back door. The footprints entered her home.

"Who goes there?" Lulu said as she cautiously stepped inside.

She followed the mysterious footprints through the hallway. To her surprise, they led into the kitchen and continued onto the counter. Lulu's curiosity grew with each step as she moved closer to uncovering the identity of her mysterious visitor.

Oddly, the footprints no longer matched one another. Each print was different in an odd way. The prints appeared to resemble different faces. "How peculiar," Lulu thought.

The scene in the kitchen was chaotic. Someone or something had made a mess; plants, roots, leaves, and stems were scattered all over the counter. The teapot was full of these plants, and two tea mugs sat nearby.

"Who goes there?" Lulu said aloud, her voice trembling with both concern and curiosity.

As Lulu followed the footprints, she found herself in the family room. The most unusual creature she had ever seen was asleep on the sofa in Lulu's favorite spot. It seemed her new neighbor was not tiny but a much larger being, soundly sleeping as peacefully as possible. Lulu tip-toed over to investigate this odd being. She noticed it had long legs and a thin frame, except its slight belly protruding beneath its clothing. This creature was unfamiliar; its face was round, with wind-blown messy hair; it looked wild, yet kind. Its nose and ears did not resemble that of a human. It appeared tired, older, with an air of gentle wisdom.

Lulu sat quietly so as not to wake it, and continued to watch as it slept. Her curiosity and imagination were high, but strangely, Lulu didn't feel afraid. She wondered if perhaps she should be more cautious. This prospective new friend appeared disproportionate with tiny feet compared to its long legs. It wasn't long before the creature awoke, looking startled as its kind eyes met Lulu's.

Lulu quickly assured the creature, "I will not cause you any harm. My home is a safe place for all who enter. Are you going to hurt me?." Lulu said. The creature relaxed and smiled. All tension just melted away. Lulu introduced herself, "I'm Tallulah. I go by Lulu. Who are you?"

"I'm called Windy. I will never hurt you," replied her new friend.

Windy the Inner-Dimensional Traveler

"Why have you come into my home, and what are you preparing in my kitchen?" Lulu asked.

"I am part of the Forgotten Realm," Windy replied. "My assignment is to care for you."

"What is the Forgotten Realm?" Asked Lulu. Her curiosity piqued.

"This is a realm where living beings can exist without fear of judgment from your world," Windy explained. "This realm of time past is a blink away. It's a special place where one can meet Lemerians, unicorns, fairies, plant spirits, ancestors, and others from different areas of the galaxy. My job is to help humans–especially humans like yourself–heal this realm. This healing encompasses the earth, the animals, and humans. Only those of pure heart are called to this forgotten place."

Lulu's mind raced as she listened, realizing that her life was about to change in unimaginable ways.

"To be a special human or to be chosen such as you, Lulu, one must understand the layers of healing for oneself and others. This also includes the animal kingdom and plant allies and the emotional connection to disease," added Windy.

Lulu, a dedicated student of herbalism who understood plant spirits and the power of living medicine, listened intently. Over the past year, she has been plagued with knee pain that no topical pain reliever or herbal remedy had alleviated. Some days, the pain was debilitating, causing her to question her expertise in her field.

"That sounds beautiful, Windy," But why do you need to care for me?" Lulu asked.

"The Forgotten Ones have invited you to travel inner-dimensionally with me," Windy replied, "to help heal your brothers and sisters and teach them about forgotten medicine. We are aware of your physical pain and the doubts you have about your depleted confidence. I am here to assist you in your healing. One must be of pure heart to travel with me, and it is clear that you are. Together, we can travel anywhere the wind goes. Does this speak to your soul, Lulu?"

Lulu's heart stirred with a mixture of excitement and hope. This was an opportunity beyond her wildest dreams, a chance to heal herself to rediscover and share forgotten healing and wisdom.

"I would love to have my pain relieved. I've dreamed of healing my brothers and sisters and being a voice for forgotten medicine. Yes! Yes! Please tell me everything, Windy," Lulu replied eagerly.

"The Forgotten Ones have been looking after you for some time now. We have taken notice of the work you have been doing here, sharing the wisdom of the plant spirits and helping those in need." Windy explained.

"I am delighted that you have chosen me. I have always enjoyed helping anyone in need, including plants and animals." Lulu said with gratitude.

"Yes, we know,'' Windy replied with a kind grin. "Your compassionate heart has not gone unnoticed. The elders have taken an interest in you. We will journey where the wind goes to meet plant spirits and help those in need."

Lulu's heart swelled with a sense of purpose. This was the beginning of an extraordinary adventure that would heal her pain and allow her to fulfill her deepest aspirations of aiding others and connecting them with the mystical realm of forgotten medicine.

"How will we get there? Car? Boat? Airplane?" Lulu asked. Her curiosity was again piqued.

Windy laughed softly and replied. "No, we will move

through space and time like the wind. You see, Lulu, I am a shapeshifter who can transform into anything desired at a moment's notice with the blessing of the Heavenly Realm."

Lulu sat in disbelief for a few moments before bursting into laughter. "Am I dreaming? How can this be possible? Perhaps I'm still asleep in my garden, she said, her voice tinged with wonder.

CHAPTER 2
THE SHAPE-SHIFTER

As Lulu sat bewildered, Windy transformed before her eyes and morphed into a beautiful, elegant, polka-dotted unicorn. Lulu's mouth gaped open in shock as she watched in amazement. The unicorn winked at her as if to say, yes, it's me. Just as quickly, Windy transformed into a rabbit, then a tiny, colorful fairy. Lulu couldn't contain her laughter at the spectacle unfolding before her. Just as quickly, Windy, her odd new friend, sat before her again.

Lulu could not help but ask, "Windy, can anyone from your realm transform themselves as you do? That was incredible."

Windy replied, "Most do channel and transform. However, The gift of shape-shifting is only for those blessed by the spirit of the elements. The gift of transformation is bestowed upon those deemed worthy and blessed by the Heavenly Realm. My gift of transformation is given from the spirit of the wind."

Lulu sat in amazement. "Embarking on a journey with a shape-shifter is remarkable, amazing, and unimaginable." Lulu expressed excitedly. "When do we begin the journey?"

"When you are ready, first you must drink the tea I have made for you. Come, and I will show you the medicinal plant allies used and how to prepare the tea to help with your ailments," said Windy.

"I'm wondering about the events in which the Forgotten Ones chose you. How did you become a part of the Forgotten Realm? Similar to how I am being chosen?" replied Lulu.

"Yes, very similar; you learn quickly," Windy said.

"Thank you for acknowledging that," Lulu responded.

"You're welcome," said Windy. "There's an old saying: the teacher appears when the student is ready. Sometimes, our teachers are not as quickly noticed. When you could see my footprints and follow them without hesitation, we felt you were ready for these introductions."

"Windy, how long have you been leaving footprints in my garden?" asked Lulu.

"A very long time," Windy said.

"Why was I only recently able to see the prints you left for me and not earlier?"

"At times, when life has been most difficult, it can appear life is going all wrong with good luck nowhere to be found. However, within the forgotten realm, we understand that we think will shape your reality. If you choose to believe that only misfortunate exists in your life, it will continue to manifest repeatedly. Recently, you experienced a shift in your thinking, surrendering to the realization that the pain you've been feeling is deeply connected to your perception of life and yourself. With your newfound awareness of your role in perpetuating your pain, you were able to shift your perspective and see the world differently. I have been leaving footprints for you for a very long time, since your early childhood, Lulu," said Windy.

"But, I have only felt this pain for the last year. What are you saying? You've been leaving your footprints for me since my early childhood. Please help me to understand."

"Lulu, don't you see that the pain in your body is part of coming into your power? This pain has been given to you to enhance your ability to see my footprints and perceive me clearly. With this clarity, you can become who you were born to become,"

"Yes, I can see that," said Lulu, "But what will I become? I've noticed that when I continually think to myself that I am always in pain and wonder if this pain will be worse than yesterday, it is not long after I begin to feel deeper pain in my body. So, when I focus on the pain, it is all I can think about. A self-fulfilling prophecy could be the catalyst that fulfills the desire to prove myself correct, I think?"

"Yes, my student, you completely understand. I am honored to call you my student, and I feel we are valuable in each other's lives. I will share any knowledge to assist your journey in healing with the Forgotten Ones in this realm and any other," said Windy.

"I am happy you are my guide and teacher. I am thrilled to be your student and excited to learn all I can from you. I feel I am being truly seen and heard for the first time in my life." exclaimed Lulu.

"At this point, Lulu, you may call me Elder Niyol," said Windy. "The transition of our relationship into student-teacher allows for you to address me by my title, bestowed upon me from the Forgotten Ones. Would you care to hear my story of how I became a shape-shifting, dimensional-traveling healer?"

"Yes, of course, Elder Niyol, I'd love to hear your story," replied Lulu.

Elder Niyol shared his story in a solemn tone. "Very well," he began, "Many moons ago, I am not certain how many, but many- I lost my father in war. My father was a samurai warrior. In those days, when the samurai lost in battle, it was only a matter of time before henchmen would come to take the lives of the remaining family members. I was just eleven years old then. Upon hearing that the henchmen were close, my mother dressed me as a girl. She told me to run and not to return, as the henchmen were looking for a boy. She then kissed me goodbye. That was the last time I ever saw her. I lost my mother that day. After wandering the country for what felt like a very long time, I eventually found work on a family farm. I have fond memories of the *spirit of the wind* guiding me along those lonesome days. The farm owners provided me food and a place to sleep, but I was treated as less than everyone else, like an animal."

Lulu's heart was filled with compassion for the young Niyol, as she watched him share his life story. Feeling honored to be in his presence, she realized he trusted her with this delicate and personal tale. She smiled gently, her expression full of warmth and empathy.

Niyol continued, "I lost myself in grief and disconnected myself from this realm. The sadness I felt was profound, and I fell into a deep depression, losing all hope and will to continue. During this time, I blamed Spirit for taking my family and lost all faith in the Heavenly Realm. To my astonishment, like you, Lulu, the Forgotten Ones arrived in my life. I also believed I was dreaming as extraordinary events unfolded before me. The father of medicine, Hippocrates, stood before me like magic. He arrived from the Forgotten Realm to heal me, just as I arrived for you."

Lulu's eyes popped open, "Hippocrates? The founding physician of the Hippocratic Oath? I shall do no harm. The guide of conduct that continues to be used by the medical profession today?" She exclaimed in disbelief, "Let food be thy medicine, and medicine be thy food."

Hippocrates 460 BC

"You are correct," replied Elder Niyol.

"Hippocrates and his student, a future Elder of the Forgotten Realm, Dr. Hahnemann, blessed me that day."

Lulu asked, "Who is Dr. Hahnemann?"

"I am sure you will have the honor of knowing him," replied Elder Niyol.

"Upon their arrival, Hippocrates reviewed my symptoms and the connection between happiness and health. He asked about my home, where I slept, my diet, my water source, my lifestyle, and how I found joy. He described himself as a holistic doctor, sharing the importance of the balance of the mind, body, and spirit connection. He asked if I had heard of him as he lived in 460 BC. He was amazed when I replied that I had heard of his work. I believe that made his day." Elder Niyol smiled.

"They had determined I suffered from deep heartbreak and grief. Hippocrates believed that grief could trigger deeper manifestations of illness. He also determined I had forgotten who I was and my purpose in this realm. He believed my spirit had become detached from my skin suit. I had also lived with terrible stomach pains, which I had endured for as long as I could remember. I did not realize they were *not* a normal part of living. The two doctors prepared a magical elixir from holy basil, St. John's wort, wood betony, and sacred water. Dr. Hahnemann prepared a potentized remedy with Thuja, which reconnects the spirit with the body. Hippocrates included the oil of black seed (Nigella sativa). I used the oil both topically and internally. The remedies were excellent at removing parasites from the body, mind, and spirit. I felt better quickly."

Lulu sat intrigued. She noticed the joy on Elder Niyol's face as he remembered his healing and time with the Healers from the Forgotten Realm.

"After my healing ceremony and initiation, I began my life as an Elder of the Forgotten Realm," Elder Niyol concluded. "Do you have any questions, Lulu?"

"Yes, many. How did the spirit of the wind choose you? How did you begin to shape-shift? Is the story finished?" Lulu asked, desiring for the sharing to continue.

"To have the gift of shape-shifting, one must live in the highest order: To do no harm and to serve the Heavenly realm," he added. "The spirit of the wind chose me because I am an ancestor of the element. My people are known as the Lyrans. The Lyrans, or lion people, existed before Earth's recorded history. My ancestors are from another galaxy, known as the Lyrae star system, from the planet Vega. They have been sending heavenly light to assist Earth in living without war and destruction for many moons. With the wind element serving as a vehicle for the heavenly light and transmissions to Earth, I can travel inner dimensionally and shape-shift with the wind, as desired. On Earth, we will use the underground travel grid, or the network of root systems, connecting the planet from one side to another." Elder Niyol smiled in completion.

"You're a Starseed teacher?" Lulu exclaimed. "I've never felt I truly belong on Earth as I do not have many friends, and I am different than most people. Am I a Starseed? How will we travel underground?"

His kind eyes met Lulu's eyes. He responded, "You will remember who you are soon enough, my student. Trust in the unknown, and all will be revealed. Let's continue our teachings as we have much to accomplish today."

"Can I ask one more question? Does your name have a special meaning?" asked Lulu.

"Yes, Niyol means *wind,* as I can travel anywhere the wind goes. Do you know the meaning of your name, Tallulah?" asked Elder Niyol.

"Yes, I do. My mother has shared my birth story with me. Within two contractions, I leaped from her waters." Lulu said with a smile. "Tallulah means one that leaps from the water. Growing up, I always had a deep affinity for water. I thrived in any activity where water was a focal point. I fondly remember attending swim meets, spending summers at beach camps, and immersing myself in activities ranging from surfing to boogie boarding. I could hold my breath and swim deeper than the other kids. These experiences by the water are some of my most cherished memories. So, how does my name connect to your arrival in my life?"

"Your name was chosen by the elders and given to your parents," Elder Niyol said. "Your connection to the water element is your strength in this life."

"Are you saying the elders knew of me before my birth,

and they gave my parents my birth name? " Lulu asked, astonished.

"You are correct again," replied Elder Niyol.

"Elder Niyol, this is a lot for me to process. Can I please have a moment to reflect on all this?" Lulu requested.

"Of course," says Elder Niyol." When you are ready, we can begin our first lesson in helping you to remove your pain and clearing yourself for inner dimensional travel."

Lulu walked to her favorite spot in the lush green enchanted garden. Bonkers, the blue jay serenaded her with a sweet melody. As she settled down and closed her eyes, she began to sift through the day's happenings—from the curious discovery of the peculiar footprints to the unexpected invitation to become a student of Elder Niyol and the Forgotten Ones. It all felt surreal, like a dream she could not escape. With a pinch to reassure herself of reality, Lulu chose to slow down the day's happenings with the holy trinity breathing meditation. She has found this practice to be very helpful in reducing stress, releasing anxiety, and more easily flowing into whatever lay ahead.

The holy trinity breathing meditation practice focuses on three deep, slow inhales through the nose with an open-mouth exhale. First, she became aware of her breath and opened up to divine guidance. She felt the rise and fall of her chest and the release of tension in her body and the muscles around her neck. With each breath, Lulu surrendered to the presence of the divine, asking for assistance in navigating life's challenges through sacred insight. She knew this sacred place of relaxation was the only place she could hear messages from God, Goddess, Jesus, the Masters of Light, and the angels.

With each inhale and exhale, she welcomed divine presence into her being. On her third breath, with a mighty lion's roar, Lulu flipped her tongue to release the weight of her worries and fears. In this state of surrender, she humbly calls upon divine guidance to assist in clarity and wisdom on this journey. She asks aloud for the ability to see, feel, and know truth through these sacred eyes. She feels the comforting presence of Spirit enveloping her and is assured of the unwavering support, even in moments of doubt and uncertainty. She embraces the profound connection with divinity with a serene smile, trusting the magical path unfolding before her.

CHAPTER 3

THE CHOSEN

After a rejuvenating self-check-in, Lulu returned to Elder Niyol, feeling clear-headed and ready for her lessons to begin. Elder Niyol had prepared a magical elixir brewed with rose petals of every color, catnip, and dandelion. Each ancient herbal ally was pure and untouched by herbicides. The Earth Mother Gaia had blessed Elder Niyol with the True Seed, a precious gift from the original time of creation. These original seeds are unadulterated and have been blessed deeply. It is mixed with sacred water drawn from the depths of the earth, where merpeople reside. This elixir holds the highest level of magic known in this realm.

Elder Niyol shared the wisdom of these magical plant healers with utmost joy and began his lessons with Lulu.

"Let's begin our lesson with the magic of the rose." He said. "Your rose garden is truly magnificent. Did you know that roses help to remove any shame connected with self-love and the love of others? They open the heart to deeper levels of vulnerability. Medicinally, every part of the rose -

its petals, hips, roots, and seeds offers excellent nutrition, including vitamin C. These nutrients are beneficial for all animals, especially humans." Elder Niyol continued. "All parts are edible and very safe. The rose has long been associated with divine feminine, such as the Holy Mother and Cleopatra of ancient Egypt. This magical herbal ally can also cleanse the blood, increase happiness, and balance excess nervousness or anxiety. Let us take a moment to smell each of these exotically colored roses."

Lulu bent down and infused her entire being with the holy spirits of the rose family. She smiled widely and breathed deeply, feeling the embrace of the Holy Mother. Overcome with emotion, a tear rolled down her face; deep emotions are often encountered with the Holy Mother's presence. She remembers the last moments she had with her own mother years prior. The memory filled her with an intense longing to be held by her mother and the Holy Mother. Lulu lost her mother to cancer. The thought of the magical herb motherwort came to her mind. Motherwort's special magic is meant to heal the heart from the loss of the feminine and the loss of family.

Elder Niyol gently touched the top of Lulu's left hand. Lulu's expression was priceless, a mix of confusion and joyful curiosity. After a moment, Lulu received coded information about the characteristics of the rose family. These codes were downloaded directly into her left hand, granting her an instant understanding of the differences between the roses' colors, actions, and personalities.

Sacred Rose

The codes downloaded:

Red Rose: With permission, can melt blocks within the heart from this life and past lives, opening one to joy, symbolize the blood shed by Jesus.

Pink Rose: Builds confidence and helps you to accept who you are entirely, allowing you to see the beautiful light you carry within yourself.

Yellow Rose: Supports calm, peace, joy, and friendship. Enhances focus on tasks and balance study, work, and playtime.

White Rose: Symbolizes innocence and the sight of purest love with spirit. Clears negative vibes and moves stagnant energy.

The Rose Family is known as the Legends of the Saints: Eternal Paradise, a link between this world and heaven.

"LET'S CONTINUE THE LESSON," said Elder Niyol. "The next magical plant healer within our elixir is catnip. Catnip is a common plant ally, also found in your enchanted garden." I'm sure you've seen cats having profound experiences with this plant spirit, as it releases hormones similar to those secreted by cats. In our elixir, catnip is used as a pain reliever as well as to reduce anxiety and elevate your spirit for inner-dimensional travel." Elder Niyol continued, "Let us breathe in the aromas of this magical plant spirit."

Lulu held catnip gently and inhaled deeply, connecting with the plant spirit. Upon opening her eyes, she saw what appeared to be a plethora of flying cats, each one a different color of the rainbow and every hue in between. The flying cats waved at her and blew her kisses. Lulu shook her head, marveling at what an extraordinary day had been. Elder Niyol noticed her reaction and gave a warm smile. He raised his hand and waited for Lulu to extend her left hand, ready to welcome the incoming codes.

The codes downloaded:

Catnip: *Revitalizes body and mind, moves stagnant energy, soothes inflammation, calms nerves, alleviates fever, and relief from ADHD. Topically- reduces pain, sprains, bruises, toothaches, and stomach aches.*

Catnip

"LET'S CONTINUE WITH THE LESSON," said Elder Niyol, "Next is the all-knowing magical dandelion. Notice that the entire plant- flower, stems, and roots— were each used in your magical elixir. Dandelion is one of the most recognized plants and is easy to grow. Notably, every part of the plant is edible, highlighting its versatility, safety, and abundance."

As the dandelions were scattered around, Elder Niyol continued his teachings. "This magic plant healer," he explained, "is used in this elixir to enhance your spiritual openness and foster trust in your ability to navigate life's challenges. Its magic proves invaluable for those who give too much of themselves and seek revitalization. Moreover, this plant is also known to be highly nutritious, encompassing all B vitamins with the ability to build and clean blood, aiding in both spiritual and physical rejuvenation. Indeed, it's one of my favorite plant healers in your realm," Elder Niyol concluded with a knowing smile.

Lulu gathered the dandelions in her arms, immersing herself in their fragrance. Instantly, she noticed the difference between the spirits of the rose family and the dandelions. While roses give a feeling of warmth and comfort, dandelions emanate a cooler sensation. The dandelions felt strong and building, and she detected a shift in vibration— a plant with the ability to rebuild one's essence. Inhaling the delightful aromas, she felt a newfound awareness of her own body. Grounded, strong, and confident, she embraced the transformative energy of the dandelions. When Lulu opened her eyes, she was amazed to see a majestic, immense lion's head before her. She roared with him, allowing his strength to emanate entirely within her soul.

Then Lulu held her left hand out, waiting to welcome the incoming codes. Elder Niyol gently touched her hand.

The codes downloaded:

Dandelion: Cleanses anger and fear, clears kidneys and bladder, helps with bedwetting, assists with everything from depression to acne, and helps one to see in the dark. Builds minerals and vitamins, halts the growth of cancer cells, and clears toxins from the blood.

DandeLion

Recipe for the magical elixir:

One mug of sacred mer-water
1 tablespoon of rose petals
1 tablespoon of dandelion; whole plant
1-1/2 tablespoons of catnip
Touch of honey, if desired
With Mortar and Pestle, open roots and stems with a gentle grinding motion
Place the material into a saucepan.
Heat the sacred mer-water - with fire; the fire shares the wisdom of the fire spirit
In a saucepan with a lid, add the roots and stems of the dandelion

With the lid on, low-boil mer-water 5 minutes
Add in flowers of rose, dandelion, and catnip leaves
Continue to simmer for 3-5 minutes
Turn off the fire, and allow the elixir to cool for 15-20 minutes
Strain and press liquid from plant material into your favorite mug
Breathe deeply, enjoy the delightful aroma of the Elixir
Enjoy & Drink as needed
Return used plant material into the earth's soil

SET INTENTIONS;

"I am ready to receive; I let go of old beliefs hindering my self-love.

I welcome the presence of Spirit;

"Let Spirit be Magnified, Make haste to deliver me, make haste to help me.

O'Lord, Blessed Be."

"Do you have any questions about the lesson, Lulu?" Asked Elder Niyol.

"Yes, I am curious about how the codes are transmuted into my body by you touching my left hand?" responded Lulu.

"Certainly, Lulu," Elder Niyol began, his voice carrying the weight of wisdom. "The codes you receive are transmuted through a sacred connection formed when I touch your left hand. It is a manifestation of ancient magic, a channel through which knowledge flows from Elder to student." Lulu, intrigued, pressed further, "But how does it work?" Elder Niyol laughed before he replied, "Ah, my dear student, it is a mystery as old as time itself. Some things are best left to the realm of magic."

"Are you ready to drink the magical elixir? This elixir will remove pain within your body," Elder Niyol explained. "During this release, you may encounter echoes of sorrow or unease as the body releases past emotions. Embrace these sensations within and release them, envisioning their departure from your skin suit. There is magic in this elixir that will facilitate your journey across dimensions, helping your body transition between realms effortlessly."

Then, Elder Niyol lit a candle and initiated a ceremony as ancient as the trees. The trees began to sway as if in response, their branches dancing in harmony. Lulu felt the wind caress her hair and skin; she couldn't help but smile, appreciating the comforting embrace of nature's warm touch. Elder Niyol extended a heartfelt welcome to Divine Spirit, invoking the presence of Heavenly Father, Heavenly Mother, Jesus, the Masters of Light, the angels, and the elemental spirits of the wind, water, earth, and fire into the sacred space they created.

Then Elder Niyol sang these words;
From near or far,
wherever you are,
please heed the call,
we'll take care of you all.
Ohhhh. Weiii.... (In a high-pitched voice)
(In spoken words)
Turner be turned,
overwind of flight,
to harm nothing within sight,

> *be free of all bindings,*
> *let only good come from this unwinding.*
> *With strength of God,*
> *take away pain,*
> *let strength remain*
> *sacred mother state my domain.*
> *Amen, and Blessed Be!*

Magical Elixir

As they both drank the mystical elixir, a profound transformation began to unfold within Lulu. In mere moments, memories of the beginning of her knee pain came flooding back. As vivid as the day they occurred. She was transported back to a serene drive through Oak Creek Canyon, renowned for its breathtaking beauty. Suddenly, her heartwarming memory crystallized around an encounter with a family of chipmunks crossing the road. In an impulse, Lulu swerved to spare the family, only to lose control of her car, skidding off the road towards the guard rail. Lulu's car had been damaged and teetered before a ten-foot drop, with the canyon far below. Yet, miraculously, the chipmunk family emerged unscathed and gratefully trotted off the roadway.

The fear that gripped Lulu at that moment was profound, resonating within her being. The injury to her knee, sustained during the harrowing accident, had lingered like a haunting shadow, refusing to relent even with time.

As the memory passed, Lulu found herself confronting the root cause of her enduring physical pain. She realized that the trauma of the accident had become entangled with a fabric of her emotions, manifesting the persistent discomfort. After the celebration of life for her mother on this day, she drove endlessly, feeling the weight of the loss of her only support system at eighteen years old.

Lulu remembered the last conversations she had with her mother, who disapproved of her friends for their preference for using stimulants over addressing the root causes of their anxiety and disharmony. Her mother had told Lulu she was better than degrading herself with their use and that her purpose was not to numb the sensations of disharmony but to address them with full authority and work through difficulties while remaining fully coherent, without stimulants. Her mother also shared that while using stimulants, whether herbal or prescribed medications, the soul of the person can be more easily influenced by unseen beings. Lulu believed her mother was losing her grip on reality and didn't realize how near her mother's passing was, nor how the cancer was spreading. In a heated argument, she had accused her mother of being too controlling and jealous, saying she wasn't spending enough time with her. Now, feeling deep remorse, she drove aimlessly, without a destination.

Lulu felt she was on the wrong timeline and path. A profound revelation dawned upon her; perhaps the appearance of the chipmunks on that faithful road was not a mere coincidence but rather a deliberate intervention orchestrated by the Forgotten Ones, nudging her life's trajectory onto a different course. After the accident, she enrolled in the School of the Healing Arts and felt aligned for the first time. Now, this unbelievable path has been shown to her, a life with the Forgotten Ones.

Yet, despite her exhaustive attempts to find relief through various supplements, the pain and emotional dysregulation persist, casting doubt upon her efficacy as a young healer and herbalist. The realization that she was unable to alleviate her own suffering had left Lulu feeling disheartened and void of belief in her abilities. But, amidst the shadows of self-doubt, Lulu found solace in the realization that this trial was not without purpose. It served as her lesson to forge deeper wisdom and self-awareness. She was determined to emerge as a better person and a more adept and apathetic healer.

As clarity dawned upon her, she surrendered herself into the embrace of the unknown, placing her trust in the guidance of Spirit and the Forgotten Ones. She realized that her journey towards healing encompassed not only physical remedies but a realization that she must forgive herself for the argument with her mother. She recognized that true healing extended beyond the confines of the physical realm, encompassing the nurturing embrace of divine guidance and spiritual support. With each passing moment, Lulu's faith in herself was rekindled as she discovered the strength and resilience buried within her soul, feeling her mother's forgiveness. She realized that such arguments were natural in loving relationships between parent and child. With her mother's spiritual support, she surrendered to the forces guiding her path. A journey of profound self-discovery and renewal lay ahead.

With a bright smile, Lulu exclaimed, "I feel clear-headed and completely at ease. My knawing anxiety is not detectable, and the knee pain is no more. What has happened? I can't believe what I am feeling. I am deeply thankful to you, thank you."

CHAPTER 4

THE INNER-DIMENSIONAL FLIGHT

"Your skin suit is now ready for flight. Let us ready yourselves and finish the remainder of the elixir. Remove your shoes and put this on. This robe is for you, as my student. This is my gift to you."

As Lulu enveloped herself in the velvety fabric she had ever encountered, she asked what material could be so smooth. Elder Niyol replied with a smile, "This fabric is created from the essence of nothing and the essence of all things. The robe will keep you grounded in your body and safe to travel through other dimensions."

They approached the ancient elder tree that had lived in Lulu's yard for as long as she could remember, known as the tree of life. The meaning "elder" came from the Anglo-Saxon dictionary, meaning "fire." Long ago, the young hollow stems of the elder were used to blow into a fire to get it burning.

"Take a seat where the roots intertwine with the soil," said Elder Niyol. "Close your eyes and follow my guidance. Together, we shall proceed with energizing your being. Are you familiar with the practice of running your energy, Lulu?"

"I believe so," she responded, "I center myself by bringing my focus to my breath, then opening the crown and root centers. I allow the flow of white angelic light to flow down from the crown and, flow up from the root, then allow the light to meet in my heart," Lulu replied. "Is this what it means to run my energy?"

"Yes, your way is wonderful," responded Elder Niyol. "I believe it will work fine with a few adjustments. Let's connect now. Just listen to my voice."

Then, Elder Niyol lit a candle and initiated a ceremony as ancient as the trees. The trees began to sway as if in response, their branches dancing in harmony. Lulu, feeling the wind caress her hair and her skin yet again, couldn't help but smile while appreciating the comforting embrace of nature's touch she remembered from before. Elder Niyol extended a heartfelt welcome to Divine Spirit, invoking the presence of Heavenly Father, Heavenly Mother, Jesus, the Masters of Light, the angels, and the elemental spirits of the wind, water, earth, and fire into the sacred space they had created.

"Bring your focus to the sound of your breath, and the beating of your heart," said Elder Niyol."

With each breath, Lulu sank deeper into relaxation. She recognized this state; relaxation was a gateway where messages from Spirit could be heard. She anticipated that this experience would surpass any sensation she had ever encountered.

Elder Niyol instructed, "Focus on three deep, slow inhales through the nose with a gentle release on each breath. Count to three in your mind. Hold for three counts with full lungs.

Release your breath for three counts. Hold empty for three counts with empty lungs. Release any tension in your shoulders, mouth, eyes, tongue, belly, legs, arms, and toes. Open the crown and root centers to allow the flow of white angelic light to meet in your heart. Keeping your eyes closed, let me know when you can see the flow of light meeting in your heart," he said. " A gentle nod is all I need."

Elder Niyol sat patiently, allowing Lulu to shift and run her energy. After a short while, Lulu gave a gentle nod. Now ready, they embark on their inner-dimensional journey.

~

ELDER NIYOL'S **guidance to connect with inner-dimensional travel:**
1. Focus on the sacred light within your heart
2. Expanding the light
3. Once the heart is connected to this sacred light, focus on expanding it until it overflows from the heart, feeling love from Spirit.
4. Concentrate on growth
5. Expand the light's growth until it fills your entire being.
6. Fill your being with angelic light
7. Surrender to wholeness -Surrender to the comforting sensations of wholeness, nourishment, and love from Spirit
8. Extend the light
9. On your next deep inhale, let the overflowing, loving, angelic light extend from beyond your physical body
10. Envelope your earthly brothers and sisters
11. Envision here a golden connective thread from person to person.

12. Extend to all beings

-Extend this angelic golden connective thread to

    the four-legged animals

    the flyers

    the crawlers

    the swimmers

13. Feel the heartbeat connection with each of them

14. Dwelling in interconnectedness

-Take deep breaths as you dwell on this heartfelt interconnectedness

-Immerse yourself in it.

-Focus on the heartfelt connection to all beings

-Feel yourself within them, ignite compassion

15. Nurture this lifelong connection

16. Once this connection is made, the connection is for life

Elder Niyol continued, "Next, visualize the plant spirits and their root systems. Please focus on the spirit of the sacred elder tree through your open heart, recognizing its root system as the highway for our journey. As you envision the inner light within these beings and feel the reciprocation of unconditional love, you will begin to see the inner-dimensional highway. This highway serves as our mode of transportation, only ignited by pure love shared between you and other beings."

Lulu followed the divine guidance of Elder Niyol. She had never felt such a deep connection to other living beings before. Her heart stirred with emotion as connection and acceptance were new to her. Soon, she felt the sensation of water flowing; whether it was the sensation on top of her skin or within her body, she could not be sure. These sensations were felt in her mind, arms, legs, and entire body.

Before she could ask how to handle these new sensations, she felt a pull, then a tug, and poof! In the blink of an eye, she felt weightless. Lulu became fluid and flowed like water. She could not make sense of the sensations she was experiencing. It was an overwhelming mix of power and fluidity as if she was both everywhere and nowhere at once.

Then, Elder Niyol sang these words:
From near or far,
wherever you are,
please heed the call,
We'll take care of you all.
Ohhhh. Weiii.... (In a high-pitched voice)
(in spoken words)
Sacred elder, tree of life
shoulder my way
protect this day.
Sun, rain, wind,
I rise and ascend,
to bend my way,
and serve each day.
Sun charge me bright,
rain cleanse my sight,
wind guide my flight
With alchemy's might
God, preserve me
AWAY WE GO...
Amen, blessed be!

Inner-Dimensional Travel Grid Network

In an instant, Lulu felt the most freedom she had ever experienced. With a whoosh, she was riding through the root system of the ancient elder tree beneath the world she once knew. She could see the thread of connection to all life forms on the planet from this inner dimension. The web of life appeared all around her, igniting with the power of the Divine Mother, Gaia, appearing as streaks of lightning. The sight was mesmerizing—a brilliant tapestry of energy and life, revealing the deep and vibrant connection that sustained all existence.

"Wahoo!" Lulu yelled. She could not contain her laughter as she flew through a dimension she knew nothing of. Lulu was beyond joy as she laughed and laughed on the ride of her life. The exhilaration of the journey filled her with an unbridled sense of wonder and delight, each moment more thrilling and surreal than the last.

"This is the first stop," said Elder Niyol, bringing their journey to an abrupt halt.

"Are you ready to meet your first healing plant spirit?" he asked.

Lulu turned to look at Elder Niyol, but he no longer appeared in front of her. His voice had changed, his face had changed, and she could not believe her eyes as he came into sharper focus.

"Jesus? Are you Jesus?" exclaimed Lulu. "Who goes there?"

CHAPTER 5

THE ELDERS

"I am him; I AM. I am a part of the inner connected web of life," replied Jesus. "Our skin suits are a part of the illusion in your world. I am part of everything, and I am the void of nothing. My presence is called forth to assure your continued connection to your heart. A pure love, unity connection is the energy that fuels the inner-dimensional grid and the ability to travel across the grid network. My purpose on earth was to assist my brothers and sisters in seeing through the clear lenses of our Heavenly Father and Heavenly Mother. To assist with sacred vision, lead with compassion for others' faults against us, and create heaven on earth through forgiveness and unity. To live a life free from the fear of judgment from others. This state of being is the divine spark necessary to maintain your inner-connectedness during travel and hold in this realm."

"Do you understand, child?" asked Jesus.

"Not quite, but I am beginning to see clearly for the first time I can remember," says Lulu. "How did you arrive here?

Help me to understand how you are standing in front of me."

"Very well," continued Jesus. "I have given my oath to serve the Heavenly Realm, just as Elder Niyol and others from the Forgotten Realm have. We can arrive at different destinations when our services are needed through the power of intention. We, the Forgotten Ones, can be channeled into any destination with the blessing of the Heavenly Realm. We channel and travel at a moment's notice to serve our oath and the Forgotten Realm effectively. I am needed, here and now, to ensure your protection and connection to the unity spark for inner-dimensional travel."

"This is the most remarkable thing I have ever witnessed," shared Lulu. "I love studying history; your life story has given me so much joy. Over the last year, I have been enthralled with your purpose and the magic you brought to Earth. I am honored to be in your presence. Will you be using your healing touch for those needing help today?"

"No, I will not," replied Jesus. "The New World is upon us, now more than any other time on earth. Your brothers and sisters must learn how to heal themselves. Moving forward, I will be a guide, sharing how the use of living medicine and a connection to the Forgotten Realm will bring about transformative healing experiences. They must realize that healing is not only of the physical body but also involves addressing the emotional traumas experienced within this life and those of their ancestors. My purpose is to guide beings into self-healing, enabling the sharing of these healing experiences from brother to sister and beyond. The true power in this realm lies in the ability to connect in unity and tell each other's healing stories without fear of judgment from your brothers and sisters."

"I understand how this new world reality will be very empowering. During my healing with Elder Niyol, I experienced exactly what you described," continued Lulu.

"Yes, child, you are a special human on Earth, only just beginning to understand who you are to become," Jesus responded.

"May I please share a memory of you? asked Lulu. "A few years ago, you appeared to me as a vision and asked why I hadn't called upon your guidance. I responded that many of those who claimed to follow you were often terribly judgmental of my choices when they differed from their own. This thought did not resonate with me and made me turn away from your guidance. You also shared that you did not need Christianity or any other religion to connect to the Heavenly Mother and the Heavenly Father," added Lulu."

Additionally, you invited me to work with you and to call on you into sacred space. Please understand that during that time, I believe I was dealing with religious trauma from my early childhood, possibly even a past life. It was after this experience that I became open to your teachings. I became enthralled with your magic, Master Teacher." Lulu expressed, then took a humble bow. "Thank you for coming to find your lost sheep, Jesus. I am eternally grateful."

Jesus replied, "I know my child. You are cared for and loved deeply." With a humble bow, he began to reveal her lost ancestry. Lulu's past life was on the sunken continent of Atlantis. She was in disbelief when he shared that she had been a prominent member of the Great Hall of the Akashic Records. Her family lineage was of noble birth; they served as caretakers of the Akashic Records and were entrusted with the most sacred of memories. The Akashic Records hold the memories of every single life a soul has lived in every realm and in every dimension of time. Lulu sat, absorbing the history of her ancestors.

Jesus smiled and asked, "Shall we continue with the lessons on the plant spirits?"

He signaled the commencement of his encounter with the ancient elder tree spirit.

Captivated by the unfolding of ancient folklore for the elder tree spirit, Lulu sat in quiet astonishment, listening to the tales of the elder tree spirit's role as the protector of the Fae realm and our own. The Fae realm is just a blink away, inhabited by fairies, sprites, pixies, leprechauns, and trolls. Lulu learned that the ancient Celtics honored this tree as sacred, symbolizing birth and death. This holy tree was never to be burned as firewood or used in woodworking due to its revered status and the dire consequences that befell those who dared to harm it. These consequences include tree limbs falling on one's home or car. The elder tree is believed to encourage prosperity, happy marriage, healthy children, protection from dark forces, and protection from lighting. The elder tree was revered as a portal to the Fae Realm in distant lands like Iceland. Lulu felt compelled to close her eyes and connect with this sacred spirit of the elder tree and the Fae Realm. In that serene moment, faint wrestling broke the silence. As she opened her eyes, a breathtaking golden-colored fairy materialized before her.

The beautiful fairy telepathically asked if she wanted to see the Fae Realm. With a nod, Lulu accepted the invitation. She asked Lulu to raise her left hand, and the lovely fairy gently touched her hand. The happenings in this forgotten realm were downloaded instantly. Lulu saw a busy little city with a water-holding tower made from rose buds and an outdoor farmers market. The merchants displayed handmade dishes made from assorted leaves and tree bark. Beautiful clothing was found in every color of the rainbow, and the merchants appeared to be insects. Caterpillars, bumble bees, flies, wasps, and gnats all seemed to get along well, focused on the duties of a merchant. Elderberries, lotus flowers, and fresh honey appeared to be their favorite treats. Lulu, again, pinched herself to be sure she was awake. She opened her eyes, and the beautiful, golden fairy laughed and asked if she was ready to continue her lesson with the great elder tree.

With their hands connected, the lovely fairy downloaded the incoming codes into Lulu's mind, racing from the sheer amount of information. The benefits of the elder tree were vast and astonishing. This download differed from the previous one, as these codes held an ancient language called Light Language. It was the most beautiful sound Lulu had ever heard - heavenly, etheric, and calming, with a sense of deep strength and inner guidance from Spirit. It was revealed that light language is accessible within the Tree of Life. These sacred sites that hold the Trees of Life are located on every continent in this realm.

The codes downloaded:

Elder Flower and Elder Berry: *Used to remove fever and induce sweating, move excess liquid or mucus caused by infection-especially in lungs, and protect from virus penetration; the sacred tree assists with chicken pox, measles, fever, gout, infection, acne, asthma, eye twitches, and pain.*

Elder Berry

LULU AGAIN SHOOK her head in amazement, recognizing how her life had entirely changed from what it had been one day before. She sat quietly, absorbing it all.

She thought I am grateful for the downloads from the Forgotten Ones and the opportunity to help others with this valuable information. Wow, this tree is truly sacred.

Lulu was called on. "Child, are you ready to journey to our next plant spirit?" Jesus appeared before her once more.

"Yes, Master Teacher, let's go," Lulu responded.

Master Jesus lit a candle and initiated a ceremony as ancient as the trees. The trees began to sway as if in response, their branches dancing in harmony. Feeling the wind caress her hair and her skin yet again. Lulu couldn't help but smile, appreciating that comforting embrace of nature's touch that she remembered from before. Jesus extended a heartfelt welcome to Spirit.

Lulu followed the divine guidance of Jesus. Soon, she felt the sensation of water flowing within her mind, arms, legs, and entire being. She felt a pull, then a tug, and poof! In the blink of an eye, she felt weightless. Lulu became fluid and flowed like water. She could not quite make sense of the sensations she was experiencing. However, she enjoyed the overwhelming mix of power and feeling free of gravity.

Then, Jesus sang these words:
From near or far,
wherever you are,
please heed the call,
we'll take care of you all.
Ohhhh. Weiii…. (In a high-pitched voice)
(in spoken words)
Burdock, you are my rock,
mullein my breath of life,
we succumb as one.
Sun, rain, wind,
I Rise and ascend,
to bend my way,
and serve each day.
Sun charge me bright,
rain cleanse my sight,
wind guide my flight,
with alchemy's might,
God, preserve me!
AWAY WE GO!
Amen, blessed be!

CHAPTER 6
THE NOTHINGNESS

In an instant, Lulu felt the freedom pulsating through her entire body. With a whoosh, she again rode through the root systems beneath the world she once knew. The sight was mesmerizing. However, Lulu noticed there was something different on this journey. She observed pockets of darkness, sensing a void as she gazed into them.

Inner-Dimensional Travel Grid Network

In an instant, she had stopped. She looks over to find

Master Jesus smiling from ear to ear. Lulu returned his gaze and smiled appreciatively.

"We are here," said Jesus, "Let us meet our plant spirits."

"We are here? Where is here?" Lulu responded.

"Master Jesus, I am curious about something I saw while riding the root system. Do we have time for a discussion?

"Of course, what is your concern?" replied Jesus.

"During our travel, I noticed areas with no light, lifeless, or just simply darkness. It looked eerie. What was that?" asked Lulu.

With a look of sorrow, Jesus responded, "Yes, child, you are right to follow your inner knowing. You have sensed the encroaching void of the *nothingness* that has been spreading rapidly within this realm. The darkness you notice is indeed what you feel; it is lifeless, devoid of light and the Spirit of Unity. Within your realm, the number of souls disconnected to spirit through light-giving, living medicine has reached its highest point ever encountered. The love of the Earth Mother and the receiving of her medicine are now at the lowest in history. The Spirit of Unity and the connective thread of light are necessary to maintain the highways within the inner-dimensional grid. Your awakening provides hope to the Forgotten Ones, strengthening their belief in the survival of this realm. Your service and commitment will inspire hope and foster the unity that is desperately needed," added Jesus.

"The areas you noticed that were devoid of light are where toxic behavior is abundant on this planet," Jesus continued. "Behaviors such as using poisons to eliminate so-called weeds and covering the earth's crust with cement hinder the root systems, clogging their flow and ability to thrive. Furthermore, the continued contribution to separation from your brothers and sisters through the act of judging one another halts the production of the connective thread of light. Thus reducing the energetic grid's existence in this realm."

Lulu listened intently, deeply saddened by the condition of her realm and the planet. "Master, I will do my very best to ensure the nothingness does not grow and become stronger," she said.

He bowed slightly and said, "Very well, my child. We will continue with the teachings, and soon, you will go through your initiation."

Lulu gave a grateful smile, bowed, and said, "What is an initiation?"

Jesus responded, "We have more plant spirits to meet. Let us go."

A short while later, Jesus said, "Here we are, child. We are fortunate to meet two ancient plant spirits; these healers are the powerful burdock root and mullein. Both grow in waste areas, along roadsides, and in damp soil. Burdock root is renowned for its blood-cleansing properties, particularly against unclean air and pollution. This magical plant spirit can be added to soups, salads, stir-fry's and even used as a coffee substitute. Its history is fascinating, as Burdock assisted the inventor of velcro, George de Mestral; he was inspired by the Burdock burrs, which stuck to his dog's fur after a walk. The hooks of velcro resemble the burrs on the burdock plant."

Lulu listened intently as she loved history and felt the purpose of each of these ancient healers in this realm.

Jesus continued, "Mullein leaf and flowers are mostly used, and the root is used occasionally. This majestic beauty has graced our realm for many, many years. Mullein has been carried in the arms of those called to her, inspiring courage, attracting sweet love, and providing protection. Children of yesterday would use the soft mullein leaves as blankets for their dolls. I like to refer to this magical plant healer as Mama Mullein."

Incredible, Lulu thought to herself. Then she said, "Why do you presume the public school system does not include the teaching of medicinal herbs?"

Jesus shrugged his shoulders with concern and said, "There are many reasons, but those who heed the call and listen will find their way. This field of study is far deeper than one can imagine, and one must be called into service to understand it properly."

"I understand, Master Jesus," said Lulu; she then raised her left hand and bowed her head, excited to receive the incoming codes of the plant spirits.

The codes downloaded:

*****Burdock Root:***** *Eliminates waste through the organs, especially the skin. Aiding in many issues, from acne, anger, cancer, hives, and staph infection to sore throat. Topically: removes ringworm.*

*****Mullein:***** *treatment of asthma, bronchitis, congestion, coughs, kidney infections, tuberculosis, and whooping cough. The flower is infused with oil to treat ear infections.*

Burdock

Mullein

Lulu sat with her eyes closed, assuring the codes were understood and stored in her memory for later use. When she opened her eyes, Jesus sat patiently, gazing at her as if she were the last hope for this realm. Then he gently asked, "Do you have any questions, my child?"

"Yes, I do. Is there a reason we have met plant spirits whose main focus has been on cold and flu symptoms," Lulu continued.

"You are a wise one indeed," Jesus acknowledged. "A young man has been sick for a long time. We will visit him after we encounter the Pasque flower, also known as Pulsatilla. The ancient plant healers we've met today will be invaluable in creating the elixir to heal him."

Lulu looked intrigued and exclaimed, "I will be able to help you heal a young man today?"

Jesus nodded with a hint of emotion as he replied, "Yes, his name is Dominic, and he and many of his brothers and sisters have been asking for his healing."

Lulu's smile widened as she said, "I too, have been asking for a teacher to help me become a more potent healer and share the powerful medicine of forgotten times. I am filled with gratitude and very excited to assist in this healing. Thank you, Jesus."

"Lulu, we have also heard your prayers, and I am equally excited. Now, let's meet our last plant spirit for today. Are you ready?" Jesus replied, his tone both encouraging and reassuring.

CHAPTER 7
THE POTENIZATION

Together, they prepared themselves for the next inner-dimensional journey. Wrapped in the most exquisite fabric, a gift from Elder Niyol, Lulu's excitement bubbled as she anticipated the ride of her life—the profound opportunity to delve into the Forgotten Ones realm as a student and assist in a healing filled her heart with awe.

Master Jesus lit a candle and initiated a ceremony as ancient as the trees. The trees began to sway as if in response, their branches dancing in harmony. Feeling the wind caress her hair and skin yet again, she couldn't help but smile. Jesus extended a heartfelt welcome to Spirit.

Lulu followed the divine guidance of Jesus. Soon, she felt the sensation of water flowing within her mind, arms, legs, and entire being. She felt a pull, then a tug, and poof! In the blink of an eye, she felt weightless and loved the sensations she felt. Away they went.

Then, Jesus sang these words:
From near or far,

wherever you are,
please heed the call,
we'll take care of you all.
Ohhhh. Weiii.... (In a high-pitched voice)
(In spoken words)
Sun, rain, wind,
I rise and ascend,
to bend my way,
and serve each day.
Sun charge me bright,
rain cleanse my sight,
wind guide my flight,
with alchemy's might,
God, preserve me,
AWAY WE GO...
Amen, blessed be!

The exhilaration of these journeys filled her with an unbridled sense of pleasure, each moment more thrilling than the last.

Inner-Dimensional Travel Grid Network

Suddenly, they came to an abrupt stop.

"We have arrived, child," said Jesus.

Lulu caught her breath and looked around. They were on a hillside. The wind was making itself known, and the colors of the flowers were vibrant. Lulu was in awe of the surrounding beauty, marveling at the purples, yellows, blues, and pinks in every hue. *'Mother Nature has outdone herself,'* thought Lulu. Jesus asked, "Lulu, have you heard of the Pulsatilla or the Pasque flower, as it is formerly known?"

"Yes, Master Jesus, I have, but very little," Lulu responded thoughtfully. "I understand that this flower is very potent and used in minimal doses. Too much of this flower can be toxic."

"Yes, this is true," responded Jesus. "You have learned much during your years on this planet. This magical plant spirit will be made into minute dosing to render any toxins ineffective. But we will discuss this a little later," he continued, delving into the folklore surrounding the pulsatilla flower. "The tales of this magical ancient healer trace back to before the time of my passing. Within the Christian tradition, this flower symbolizes my resurrection from the tomb after my physical death. It embodies perseverance in the face of death and serves as a reminder when passion has been taken too far. Further, the myth suggests that this flower grows in places that had been soaked by the blood of the ancient Romans, as its growth is mainly found in old barrows and hillsides."

Lulu gazed across this beautiful hillside, imagining a time when Jesus walked this earth. The impact he made was undeniable, shaping not only history but even the way we measured time itself, with his birth marking the beginning of the AD era. She pondered the meaning of AD and BC while reflecting on the timeline of this realm. Then she asked Master Jesus, "What is the meaning of AD and BC?"

"Before Christ is the meaning of BC, a time before my day of birth on Earth," Jesus responded. "This term is used worldwide; regardless of the language spoken, it remains universal. The meaning of AD is 'Anno Domini,' which means 'in the year of the Lord.' This refers to the year I was born, while my death is believed to have occurred in 33AD, as I passed over at the age of thirty-three."

Jesus & Pulsatilla Flowers

Lulu was grateful; she enjoyed learning about history. She recognized how her passions had been helpful in her journey as a student of the Forgotten Ones.

As Jesus approached Lulu, she bowed respectfully, ready to receive the incoming codes of the plant spirits. Standing in anticipation, she suddenly heard a rustle and opened her eyes to find a tall, slender man standing before her. He was partially bald, with white hair, and had deep lines etched into his face. He exuded an air of an aristocrat of times long past.

Lulu greeted the unfamiliar figure with a smile and asked, "Who goes there?"

The man responded with a confident tone, "My name is Dr. Samuel Hahnemann. I am the founding father of Homeopathy. My time on this planet was between 1755 and 1843. I am a German physician, chemist, and writer. I am fluent in five languages and have been a translator and teacher of each. I have been channeled here to further your lessons."

Lulu pleasantly responded, "Pleasure to meet you, Dr. Hahnemann. Are you the same doctor who healed Elder Niyol?

"Yes, I am the same doctor who assisted Hippocrates in healing Elder Niyol. I am a part of the Forgotten Ones, sent here to present a lesson on Homeopathy," said Dr. Hahnemann. "Please let us sit and make ourselves comfortable."

They both sat in the grass, surrounded by the bounty of the pulsatilla flowers. Dr. Hahnemann breathed deeply, savoring the aroma. He gazed over the countryside, taking notice of the remarkable colors that Earth Mother had in her color palette. Then he said, "Shall we begin your lesson?"

"Yes," replied Lulu. "May I ask a question, Doctor?"

"Of course," Dr. Hahnemann responded.

"How did you create homeopathy? What was your motivation? How did you first come to the idea of this medicine?" Lulu asked.

"Well, it seems you are a mind-reader," responded the doctor, "as this is what our first lesson will be focused on."

"The angels bestowed upon me a vision. One evening, in 1796, I was very unhappy with the state of medicine, as the physicians resorted to bloodletting or injecting liquid mercury, which I believed sometimes did more harm than good," explained Dr. Hahnemann, "My sense of duty and the Hippocratic Oath that said 'I shall do no harm' would not allow me to treat unknown causes of suffering for my brothers and sisters in this manner. During this vision, the angels revealed the method of potentizing remedies through succession. We'll delve deeper into this shortly. Driven by an intense sense of duty to humanity, I stopped practicing medicine altogether and dedicated myself to the pursuit of chemistry and writing. This continued until the evening the angels gave me the vision."

As Lulu sat captivated, she realized this was no ordinary doctor; he was a master healer brought to her by the Forgotten Ones. Curiosity stirred her as she wondered if the Forgotten Ones were all Masters of Healing. Intrigued, she remained seated in silence, feeling deeply honored to be in his presence.

Dr. Hahnemann continued, "Homeopathy was founded on the principle of 'like cures like.' For instance, when a remedy administered to a healthy individual induces symptoms similar to the disease, it becomes the chosen remedy —this is 'like cures like.'" He explained further, "Remedies are made using a vast array of substances, ranging from elemental silver and gold to various plants, spanning from non-toxic to toxic, as well as the animal kingdom including bees and spider venom. Through the process of dilution, homeopathy achieves heightened effectiveness and removes toxins from a 'poisonous' substance. This is in stark contrast to conventional medicine, where higher doses of the drug may aggravate the illness. I discovered that dilution, coupled with the action of potentization and minute dosing, to be quite successful," concluded Dr. Hahnemann.

Lulu appeared bewildered as she inquired, "Can you explain the concept of potenizing a remedy? And exactly what does dilution entail?"

"Of course, I can," said Dr. Hahnemann. "Dilution is just

as it sounds; essentially, we are watering it down from its original form. To understand potentization, we must talk about succussion. Both processes alter the energy of the remedy, intensifying its potency. This is achieved by shaking the bottled remedy up and down, landing upon the Holy Bible, thus creating an elevated vibrational frequency."

Lulu gazed at Dr. Hahnemann as if he were speaking a language different than English. She couldn't help but smile, her grin stretching from ear to ear, "Doctor," she responded, "is this the wisdom the angels shared during their visit? This is unlike anything I've ever heard."

"Indeed, and there's so much more," replied Dr. Hahnemann. "The knowledge and wisdom I am sharing is elementary, my dear. These angels enlightened my life and enabled me to perceive medicine beyond this dimension. Through the practice of succussion and the elevation of frequencies within remedies, I've ignited the deepest parts of the mind, body, and spirit. This level of deep healing cannot be accomplished without the guidance of Spirit."

Dr. Hahnemann smiled, recognizing the challenge of grasping these concepts. "We'll explore these principles further in our future lessons," he assured. "But for now, Lulu, do you have any questions?"

Lulu sat quietly, in deep thought, carefully processing the information. After a moment, she responded, "No, I do not have any questions. Thank you, Doctor."

Lulu knowingly raised her left hand and eagerly anticipated the transmission of the incoming codes from the plant spirits. Dr. Hahnemann gently touched her left hand, and in that moment, the codes flowed into her like water.

Pulsatilla Codes Downloaded:

An acrid taste may burn the tongue and throat and cause

blisters on the skin. Used external remedy for ulcers and inflamed eyes and used with bad breath, discharges; mucus—thick; yellow, green, bland. Lips and mouth are dry, without feeling thirsty. Glands are swollen, tongue coated white/yellow. Loves walking in the fresh open air, and easily cries then laughs. Dislikes: fatty foods, heat, and stuffy rooms. Coughs: return in a stuffy room, constant during the evening, dry at night, violent and wracking, disturbs sleep, and may have nausea after a coughing fit. Due to the toxic effects, it is better used within Homeopathy; it's safe and effective.

Homeopathy Codes Downloaded:

A system that was founded on the stated principle that "like cures like," similia similibus curantur, and which prescribed drugs or other treatments for patients that would produce symptoms of the diseases being treated in healthy persons.

In homeopathy, potency refers to the levels of dilution of the substance used to make a remedy. For instance, a potency of 6X indicates that the substance has been diluted and shaken vigorously (succussed) six times. Similarly, a potency of 30C means that it has been diluted and shaken vigorously (succussed) 30 times.

Remedies with a potency of up to 6X are classified as having a very low potency. These remedies closely resemble the original state, predominantly affecting the physical or material level by attaching to specific tissues and organs. High potencies act for longer durations and penetrate more profoundly, whereas low potencies act for shorter durations and have a more superficial impact.

The 200c and above levels are higher potency. Higher potencies effectively influence an individual's emotional and psychological state.

In cases of acute illness, regular administration of remedies is necessary to effectively counteract the progression of the illness.

The remedy should be taken at a frequency sufficient to maintain a stable response and should be adjusted as the illness's intensity decreases.

For intense symptoms, a dose should be taken every 15 minutes for the first hour; upon improvement, the frequency of administration should be reduced to hourly.

~

ONCE THE INFORMATION download was completed, Lulu opened her eyes, inhaled, and shook her head in amazement. She felt the most magical medicine she had ever experienced.

Dr. Hahnemann smiled and confidently said, "This is amazing, is it not?"

"I am in astonishment; thank you for the healing you have brought to earth. You are no ordinary doctor," Lulu said warmly.

"Do you have any further questions?" asked Dr. Hahnemann.

"Yes, but right now, my mind is ecstatic. I'll ask later," Lulu replied.

"Very well then, let's be off to heal our patient," Dr. Hahnemann responded.

"Is this Dominic?" asked Lulu.

"Yes, the very same," replied Dr. Hahnemann.

Lulu gathered her sacred robe and prepared for their journey. Jesus magically appeared before her. Channeled into the here and now to ensure her protection and unified connection to the travel network.

Wrapped in her favorite fabric, Lulu's excitement bubbled as she again anticipated the ride of her life. Master Jesus lit a candle and initiated the ancient ceremony. The trees began to sway as if in response, their branches dancing in harmony. Lulu felt the wind caress her hair and skin yet again.

Jesus extended a heartfelt welcome to Spirit.

Lulu followed the divine guidance of Jesus. Soon, she felt the sensation of water flowing within her mind, arms, legs, and entire being. She felt a pull, then a tug, and poof! In the blink of an eye, she felt weightless and ready for her flight. Away they went.

Then, Jesus sang these words:
From near or far,
wherever you are,
please heed the call,
we'll take care of you all.
Ohhhh. Weiii.... (In a high-pitched voice)
(in spoken words)
Sun, rain, wind,
I rise and ascend,
to bend my way,
and serve each day.
Sun charge me bright,
rain cleanse my sight,
wind guide my flight,
with alchemy's might,
God, preserve me,
AWAY WE GO...
Amen, blessed be!

The Nothingness

They swished and whooshed through the underground system, both smiling ear to ear, laughing with pure excitement. It wasn't long before they came upon the *nothingness,* alarmed to see that the area had grown larger. Both looked on with deep concern, and all laughter stopped.

CHAPTER 8
THE HEALING

"We are here," said Dr. Hahnemann.

Lulu glanced over and warmly smiled. Jesus was no longer present, and the good doctor was before her. Lulu felt comforted by the blessed Doctor and eager to learn all she could from him. Dr. Hahnemann returned her gaze with a bright smile and said, "Are you ready to meet Dominic?"

"Yes, absolutely," replied Lulu.

They approached a young man of perhaps fifteen years old, sitting quietly in a wheelchair; Lulu followed behind the Doctor and listened intently. Dominic sat outside in his garden under a beautiful weeping willow tree. He gazed at them both and asked, "Am I dreaming?"

"No, sir, I am Dr. Hahnemann, and this is Lulu, a future Elder in training. We are before you today, and this is not a dream."

Dr. Hahnemann gave a wink to Lulu and continued, "Please stay seated, Dominic. This spot under the weeping willow is outstanding for your healing."

Dominic looked shocked. He felt confused.

"Are you the same Dr. Hahnemann who created the Homeopathic medicine system.?" he asked.

"Yes, sir, I am the very same person. How do you know of me and homeopathy?" Dr. Hahnemann replied.

"Well, Dr. Hahnemann, I have not been well for a long time, and recently, homeopathy came up in a Google search under effective supplements for chronic cough," replied Dominic. "I then researched the origin of homeopathy and discovered your incredible healing system and life history. You passed over in Paris, France, on July 2, 1843. How are you standing before me, and how did you arrive here? I don't see a car." Dominic asked as if he lost his breath.

"We have heard your prayers and those of your family and friends," replied Dr. Hahnemann. "We have come to answer your prayers. The realm of the Forgotten Ones and the Heavenly Realm has sent us. We serve Spirit, humanity, and many other beings in this realm." Dr. Hahnemann continued. "We can answer more of your questions later, but let's begin your healing for now. May we use your kitchen to prepare the medicine?"

"Yes, of course, but I'm still confused about all this," he said in a weak voice,

Dr. Hahnemann reviewed his symptoms. "Dominic, please nod if I have your symptoms correct. You have had this illness for over nine months. You feel better in fresh air. You cough more in the evenings, and your mouth and lips lack moisture, yet you desire no liquids. The cough is hacking, and at times, you cannot stop coughing; you have vomited during coughing, as well as cracked your left lower rib. Your body temperature is in constant fluctuation. Is this correct?" Dr. Hahnemann finished.

Dominic gave a gentle nod to confirm his symptoms.

"Very well, young man, please stay where you are. We will return shortly,"

Lulu and the doctor readied the magical elixir; they boiled fresh spring water from the realm of the merpeople and added the magical herbal spirits of Burdock root. After a few minutes, they gently added Mama Mullein's delicate leaves and flowers and the wise spirits of the Elderflowers and Elderberries. Once the elixir was prepared, they allowed the liquid to cool and then strained the plant particles from the liquid. Some of the elixir would not keep, so they stored what they could for later use in cold storage.

Next, they prepared the pulsatilla flower using a liquid dilution that Dr. Hahnemann carried with him. They filled a small glass vial with the dilution of pulsatilla and began the succussion process. Dr. Hahnemann pulled from his bag a beautifully bound, golden book. The book read *Hahnemann Family Holy Bible* and displayed the family crest on the cover. The book was ancient, belonging to many generations before him. Dr. Hahnemann held the vial of pulsatilla between his pointer finger and thumb, bringing it up and down, striking it against the Holy Bible. He repeated this process over a hundred times. The more a remedy was succussed, the deeper the medicine would heal the emotional body. Dominic had been sick for an extended period, and his emotional body was exhausted. Therefore, the medicine was succussed at higher levels. The greater the dilution and potentiation, the less of the actual ingredient remained, but the medicine became stronger and carried a higher level of frequency.

Lulu helped where she could but felt better suited to watch, ask questions, and absorb the incredible process of medicine-making she was witnessing.

Recipe for the magical elixir:
One mug of sacred mer-water
1 tablespoon of Burdock root
1 tablespoon of Mullen flowers & leaves
1 tablespoon of Elder flowers & Elderberries
touch of honey, if desired
With mortar and pestle, open roots and stems with a gentle
grinding motion
Place the material into a saucepan
Heat sacred mer-water - with fire; the fire shares the
wisdom of the fire spirit
In a saucepan with a lid, add the roots and stems of the
burdock
With the lid on, low-boil mer-water 5 minutes
Add in flowers and stems of mullein, elder, and elderberries
Continue to simmer for 3-5 minutes
Turn off the fire, and allow the elixir to cool for 15-20
minutes
Strain and press liquid from plant material into your
favorite mug
Breathe deeply and enjoy the delightful aroma of the Elixir.
Drink as needed
Used plant material - mix with Castrol Oil and Eucalyptus
oil for poultice

Homeopathy; Pulsatilla - succussed over 100 times
1 drop under the tongue, 15-minute intervals as needed
for one hour
Reduce the dose as symptoms are relieved
Set intentions;
"I am ready to receive; I let go of old beliefs hindering
my self-love.
I welcome the presence of Spirit;

"Let Spirit be Magnified, make haste to deliver me, make haste to help me.

O'Lord, Blessed Be."

∽

WITH THE ELIXIR and pulsatilla in hand, they returned to Dominic under the weeping willow tree. Dr. Hahnemann quietly greeted his sleeping patient and handed him a warm cup of the magical elixir.

"Dominic," Dr. Hahnemann said with a kind smile, "this elixir is taken one cup thrice daily. You will drink it until the supply in cold storage is finished."

Dominic looked up with a soft smile and began to drink. Next, Dr. Hahnemann mixed the herb combination strained from preparing the elixir with castor oil and eucalyptus oil, then applied the mixture as a poultice over Dominic's lungs. Dominic smiled and commented on how good it felt. Finally, Dr. Hahnemann administered the Pulsatilla.

"Will you please open your mouth? I will place one drop of the pulsatilla remedy under your tongue," said Dr. Hahnemann. "Just allow the remedy to melt gently in your mouth. We will administer the Pulsatilla every fifteen minutes, then adjust the dose depending on your level of well-being."

Dr. Hahnemann then turned to Lulu, saying, "Let's prepare for the spiritual healing. Place Dominic here, where the weeping willow's roots meet the earth."

Lulu nodded and followed the instructions.

"Dominic, can you come off your wheelchair and lie down on the earth? Lulu will help you," Dr. Hahnemann asked.

Dominic nodded and slowly came down from the chair onto a cozy, soft pile of blankets and pillows Lulu had prepared.

Dr. Hahnemann continued, "For this healing portion, I will guide you into a sacred place and run your energy. Do you have any experience with this?"

"No, doctor. But I will do as I am guided," replied Dominic.

Lulu and Dominic heard a faint rustling, and as they glanced over to Dr. Hahnemann, they saw a different person with long, dark hair standing with his back to them.

"Who goes there?" said Dominic.

The stranger turned to face them, and Lulu shouted, "Jesus, Master Teacher, I have missed you."

Jesus gave a warm smile and a kind bow. Dominic appeared shocked, completely speechless, and utterly confused.

"How are you standing here, Master Jesus?" Said Dominic

"I have been channeled into the here and now through the power of intention. I am needed here to assist with your spiritual awakening. The Heavenly Realm requested my presence. Now, it is time for your next dose of Pulsatilla. Lulu, please administer the remedy. One drop under the tongue, my child." Jesus said.

"Yes, of course," replied Lulu.

"What just happened? Who? What? How?" Dominic asked as he began to cough.

"My child, I am here to show you how to heal yourself," replied Jesus, "We are a part of the Forgotten Realm."

"What is the Forgotten Realm?" Dominic inquired. "I have heard this term a few times now."

"This is a realm where living beings can exist without

fear of judgment from your world," Jesus explained. "This realm of time past is just a blink away. It's a special place where one can meet Lemerians, unicorns, fairies, plant spirits, ancestors, and others from different areas of the galaxy. Many of the healers, known and unknown, are within this realm. Only those of pure heart are called to this forgotten place. You are of pure heart, Dominic."

"You see, Dominic, I am able to be channeled and transform at will. With the blessings of the Heavenly Realm, I can arrive in the here and now at a moment's notice. This ensures the delivery of my promise, my Hippocratic Oath; to do no harm and serve the Heavenly Realm." Jesus continued. "Do you have any further questions, my child?"

"I've been having dreams of you visiting me, Jesus; I am grateful to be in your presence," replied Dominic. "I understand and feel blessed."

"Let's move forward so you can witness and share your healing story. Sit back and allow your body to relax and unwind. During this healing, you may experience emotions and memories that come into focus. Acknowledge their meaning, then release them into the hands of the Heavenly Mother and the Heavenly Father. Close your eyes now. Focus on the sacred Christ light within your heart. Once your heart is connected to this sacred light, focus on expanding the light until it overflows from your heart, filling you with love from the Holy Spirit. Surrender to the comforting sensations of this love, and feel nourished, connected to all beings."

"Lulu, my child, would you like to guide us this time?" Jesus asked.

She looked uncertain, but Jesus smiled and said, "I would not have asked if I did not think you were ready for the task."

"Very well, I would be honored," Lulu responded.

She immediately felt butterflies in her stomach, feeling unconfident with this task, but she continued. Lulu knowingly lit the blessed candle and initiated the ceremony. The trees began to speak to her, and the wind began to sing to her as if, in response, the elements seemed to come alive. The fire and wind elements led the way, and the earth beneath her began to soften. She felt the wind caress her hair and skin. She smiled, loving the connection and the feeling of unity. Lulu extended a heartfelt welcome to Divine Spirit, invoking the presence of Heavenly Father, Heavenly Mother, the Masters of Light, the angels, and the elemental spirits of the wind, water, earth, and fire into the sacred space she created.

Then, together, Jesus and Lulu sang these words;
From near or far,
wherever you Are
please heed the call,
we'll take care of you all.
Ohhhh. Weiii.... (In a high-pitched voice)
(in spoken words)
Turner be turned,
be free of all bindings,
let only good come from this unwinding.
remove the cough,
from on to off.
Amen, Blessed Be!

~

DOMINIC FELT a profound transformation begin to unfold. In mere moments, memories of the beginning of his illness came flooding back. As vivid as the day they occurred, he was transported to a heated disagreement with his mother. The conflict escalated; he and his mother said terribly mean things to one another and had not spoken since the incident. Shortly after, he moved out of his mother's home and into his father's. While he cherishes living with his father, the disconnect from his mother has brought him deep sadness and grief. Despite his mother's attempts to repair their relationship, he had not accepted her apologies.

As the memory passed, Dominic found himself confronting the root cause of his enduring illness. He realized that the trauma of the incident had become entangled with a fabric of his emotions, manifesting as persistent discomfort and grief rooted in the lungs. A profound revelation dawned upon him. Perhaps the appearance of Jesus and Lulu held a deeper meaning than his healing. Who were the Forgotten Ones? How did Dr. Hahnemann shift his body into that of Jesus? Perhaps this illness was no mere coincidence but rather a deliberate intervention orchestrated by the Forgotten Realm, nudging his life's trajectory into a different course. Jesus said I will be sharing this story with my brothers and sisters. Perhaps I'm to give others hope on their healing journeys.

Dominic seemed to find solace in the realization that perhaps this illness was not without purpose. It could have served as a catalyst through which he could forge a deeper understanding of wisdom and forgiveness. Embracing this challenge with the surrender into the hands of spirit, he was determined to emerge as a better person and a better son. His longing for his mother was at its most intense. "Forgive" was the only word that his mind could hear. Then, he heard, "Be kind and compassionate to one another, forgiving each other, just as Spirit has forgiven you. Do not judge, and you will not be judged. Do not condemn, and you will not be condemned. Forgive, and you will be forgiven."

Dominic reviewed the events with his mother, realizing he had judged her unfairly and condemned her publicly. As this clarity dawned upon him, he realized he was accountable for his actions and felt an urgency to ask for forgiveness from her. He surrendered into the embrace of the unknown, placing his trust in the guidance of Spirit and the Forgotten Ones. He realized that his journey toward healing encompassed physical remedies and a profound connection to the spirit realm. True healing, he recognized, extended beyond the physical realm, embracing divine guidance and spiritual support. Dominic's faith in himself was rekindled with each passing moment he discovered the latent reservoirs of strength and resilience buried within his soul. As he sifted through the layers of accountability in the unfortunate argument with his mother, he felt the surrender and trust in Spirit.

Dominic awoke with a feeling of completeness. He took a full breath in, noticing there was no cough. He smiled, feeling the urgent need to connect with his mother, heal the ancestral trauma, and clear any future karmic cycles.

CHAPTER 9

THE INITIATION

Dominic opened his eyes and met the eyes of Jesus. He thought; The world's most renowned healer is before me. I must be blessed. He was amazed. Then he glanced over at Lulu, the upcoming Elder, and wondered, How did this young girl become selected for such an incredible life?

Dominic began to laugh, unable to believe what he'd just witnessed. Lulu joined in, and then Jesus joined with a deep belly laugh. Suddenly, a sweet, tiny voice chimed in. Pop! The beautiful golden fairy appeared out of nowhere, laughing along with everyone.

Dominic heard a sound similar to a horse's whinny. POP! A polk-a-dotted unicorn materialized out of thin air. Dominic could not contain his joy as the magic continued to unfold, filling the air with heightened energy of laughter and unity with the surrounding beautiful souls.

The polk-a-dotted unicorn laughed so hard that he began to pass gas, propelling himself uncontrollably. From one side of the yard to above the weeping willow tree, he landed next to Dominic. Each one rolled with laughter. Lulu was in bliss and intrigued with the magic being displayed.

At that moment, a most euphoric and beautiful voice filled the air. The voice was mesmerizing, singing ancient words of love known as light language. The enchanting music touched Dominic's soul deeply, opening his heart. Dominic followed the voice up above to the branches of the weeping willow, where an apparition of the Holy Mother appeared, surrounded by angels. Their singing was so beautiful that the laughing ceased, and all eyes watched joyfully.

Lulu and Dominic sat in pure delight and utter amazement. Before long, they felt the purity of their hearts and heard on the wind that they were forgiven and protected. Soon, tears began to roll down their faces. The overwhelming rush of emotions was common when the Holy Mother appears, as many report uncontrollable tears of joy. Feeling a profound love they had never experienced, their hearts softened as they received the abundance of codes from Heaven and the Holy Mother above.

Then the Holy Mother spoke, "Dominic, we are here to bless you and to help you remember who you are and the importance of connections to our parents. Do not allow the influences of modern times to affect your actions. Remember who you are; you are light, you are love, you are the child of the Heavenly Father. Judgments are not for this realm; they are left for the Father at the time when you leave this realm. Surrender. Live in love. Live in gratitude. Live in compassion. Live with forgiveness. Stand in your remembrance, and love yourself."

With a calm demeanor, Dominic bowed his head, knowing he was in the presence of the most sacred of all beings, and wept.

"Lulu," the Holy Mother continued, "you are blessed, my child. Your family lineage has been forgotten, erased from your mind. We will help you remember your ancestors. You have proven yourself in the eyes of the Forgotten Ones. It is time for your initiation to begin. Stand, my child."

Jesus also stood with her as Dominic looked on in amazement. Dominic realized that he hadn't coughed once during the laugh circle. Smiling through his tears, he felt an overwhelming surge of gratitude.

Lulu stood, unsure of her worthiness but trusting in the blessings of the Holy Mother and the Forgotten Realm. She found reassurance in her abilities. Jesus placed his hands over her head and asked her to close her eyes. Barefoot and draped in the blessed robe, Lulu obeyed, surrendering to the unknown and into the hands of Spirit. At that moment, her beloved teacher and guide, Elder Niyol, appeared. They spoke these words together with Jesus, the Holy Mother, the angels, the spotted unicorn, and the tiny fairy.

Romans 12:1-2-2

"Do not conform to the pattern of this world, but be transformed by renewing your mind to approve God's perfect will."

The ceremony commenced, and the trees waved in joyful fun. Their branches danced with the wind. Lulu felt the elements bless her with strength. She released any doubt of her worthiness for this Initiation. All those present felt the sacred space being created.

Jesus, the Holy Mother, the angels, the spotted unicorn, the tiny fairy, and Elder Niyol sang from ancient melodies. Somehow knowing the words, Lulu began to speak as if she had always known this timeless ceremony.

Lulu noticed moisture around her feet as if the earth

had experienced heavy rain. She welcomed the spirit of the water and eagerly continued with her Initiation.

Holy Mother

-They Sang-
Psalm 51:10-12:
"Create in me a clean heart, O God
And put a new and right spirit within me"
(Spoken words)
I stand in circles of light,
Let nothing shield my might,
Beyond the grass, my light began,
into heaven my light has ran.
Sacred Waters of Forgotten Realms,
I rise & ascend.
Sacred water change me,
sacred earth support me,
sacred wind guide me,
sacred fire ignite me.
God Preserve Me!
Amen, Blessed Be!
I see thee!

~

DOMINIC SAT, watching intently as the magic continued to unfold. Jesus dropped his hands to his side while Lulu looked around, bewildered at what transpired. Soon, Lulu felt the sensation of water flowing within her mind, arms, legs, and entire being. She felt a pull, then a tug, and poof! In the blink of an eye, she felt weightless. The feeling was remarkable; there was no tension, and she was completely untethered and free from all bindings.

However, the sensations were different than before. She no longer felt her body; her skin suit had disappeared. She had fully merged with the water element, memories of past lives in Atlantis came flooding into her. The *spirit of the water* spoke to her. She heard these words in a thundering voice that shook her very essence.

"Allow magic to happen, and it will, my child. Many realms exist side by side, rubbing shoulders with each other; one realm will continue daily, unaware of the others. In this realm, the inhabitants are in constant struggle and desire for power, driven by gluttony. In other realms, perhaps on different planets, there is only grace and the desire to create and express without fear of judgment. You can feed the nothingness, or you can become a creator. Which realm do you choose, Lulu?"

Lulu thought deeply and replied, "I will take my sacred oath and protect against the *nothingness*. I will create a realm free of judgment; I am a creator. I will serve the Forgotten Realm with the blessings of the Heavenly Realm." Her heart fluttered in acknowledgment of her self-empowerment.

She realized that she retained her ability to see, hear, and feel through the transformation. She could see Jesus, the Holy Mother, the angels, the spotted unicorn, the tiny fairy, Dominic, and Elder Niyol looking right at her. Could they see her? Could they hear her? What had happened?

From the depths of the earth, the water rose higher and higher until they were completely submerged. The Holy Mother and Jesus exchanged knowing smiles, acknowledging the events about to unfold. Lulu realized this water had risen from the deepest part of the earth, the realm of merpeople, a place of utmost serenity. This water held the highest level of magic and is the most sacred. Elder Niyol and Dr. Hahnemann had used the same sacred water to prepare the magical elixirs.

The enchanting sounds of music in every direction enveloped them, an entire symphony of angelic music vibrating within this sacred water. Lulu and Dominic gazed at the spectacular display of beauty. Dancing seahorses appeared, followed by what seemed to be mermaids and mermen. Dominic glanced at Lulu, who was grinning from ear to ear. The merpeople approached her. Instinctively, she bowed. The queen of the mer-realm stepped forward, reached out, and gently touched her hand, igniting incoming codes. As far as the eye could see, merpeople touched each other's shoulders, linking the current of the download flowing into Lulu's hand.

Lulu felt like she was in a dream, wondering how they could see her when she had been water a while ago. Looking down at her skin suit, she saw a beautiful, golden mer-tail floating gently where her legs had once been. She also noticed the ease of breathing underwater and then realized they had been communicating telepathically all along. "Wow, what an extraordinary day," she thought. "I'm a mermaid."

Lulu raised her head to gaze at the MerQueen. Her jaw dropped in astonishment, feeling overwhelmed by the incoming codes. Her family lineage came rushing into remembrance— her ancestors were indeed from the lost continent of Atlantis, making their way as Merpeople. One by one, each mermaid and merman stepped forward to meet her. The MerQueen was the last to speak with her. She was invited to study with the MerQueen as part of her training to become an Elder of the Forgotten Realm.

Queen of the MerPeople

Gazing and smiling at the most beautiful being she had ever met, the Queen. Lulu responded telepathically, "I would be honored to study with you and prepare to become a future Elder and member of the Forgotten Realm." She bowed in deep gratitude.

Lulu rose to see a floating paper scroll and a pen before her. She pulled the scroll open and was presented with the 'Hippocratic Oath' in its entirety. At the bottom of the scroll was a list of signatures from times past. The first signature was none other than Hippocrates, the father of medicine himself. Her heart fluttered. The signatures continued with many more; Mary Magdelene, Jesus Christ, Dr. Samuel Hahnemann, Windy Sisson, Renee Cassie, Dr. Usui, Dr. Wilhelm Schuessler, Gautama Buddha, Maitreya, St. Michael, Zarathustra, Moses, Melchizedek, Mother Mary, St. Frances, St. Germain, El Morya, Therese of Lisieux, Kuthumi, Serapis Bey, Paul the Venetian, Hilarion, Lanto, Quan Yin and many more.

Lulu signing the Hippocratic Oath

Lulu gazed upward, fully absorbing the moment. Taking a deep breath, she met the eyes of the Holy Mother. The Holy Mother bowed her head, invoking the sacredness of the moment. Jesus joined in the bow, followed by the mermaids and mermen. The seahorses followed suit, with the MerQueen folding into the most profound bow of them all. She gently picked up the pen and signed her name alongside the list of Healers, taking the most sacred oath: to serve and to do no harm under the guidance of the Heavenly Realm.

Lulu wondered if all those on the list could transform

and shape-shift. Could each member of the Forgotten Realm travel inner-dimensionally? Did each name on the list know of the Forgotten Realm? How is she related to the merpeople? She had many questions for the MerQueen.

Intoxicating, enchanting music seemed to come from every direction, growing more intensely. Heavenly light in hues of gold and white appeared from above, below, and all around. She felt connected in unity to all beings, which further melted her heart, inspiring her to sing along. All those present began to sing in beautifully sacred and lovely tones, harmonizing as if they had sung together many times before. From the core of her being, Lulu sang, unsure of how she knew these words but believing the light codes were part of the download from the MerQueen. Each held the hand of the other, connecting in the Spirit of Unity and reestablishing the threads of light.

Together they sang:
O'lord of the brightest light
Know me and hold me tight
Show me the way that's right
O'lord, O'lord, O'lord
O'lord, O'lord, O'lord
Guide me with all your might
O'lord come to guide our fight
O'lord, O'lord, O'lord
O'lord, O'lord, O'lord
Guide me into your light
O'lord of the brightest light
O'lord, O'lord, O'lord
hmm, hmm, hmm
(Song Title: Into the Light)

The inner-dimensional travel grid network pulsed with high vibrational frequencies.

Stay Beautiful! Volume II is on its way.

Into the Light

By Rhea Iris Rivers

The Hippocratic Oath
460 BC

I swear by Apollo the physician, and Aesculapius, and Health, and All-heal, and all the gods and goddesses, that, according to my ability and judgment, I will keep this Oath and this stipulation—to reckon him who taught me this Art equally dear to me as my parents, to share my substance with him, and relieve his necessities if required; to look upon his offspring in the same footing as my own brothers, and to teach them this Art, if they shall wish to learn it, without fee or stipulation; and that by precept, lecture, and every other mode of instruction.

I will impart a knowledge of the Art to my own sons, and those of my teachers, and to disciples bound by a stipulation and oath according to the law of medicine, but to none others.

I will follow that system of regimen which, according to my ability and judgment, I consider for the benefit of my patients, and abstain from whatever is deleterious and mischievous.

I will give no deadly medicine to any one if asked, nor suggest any such counsel; and in like manner I will not give to a woman a pessary to produce abortion.

With purity and with holiness I will pass my life and practice my Art.

I will not cut persons laboring under the stone, but will leave this to be done by men who are practitioners of this work.

Into whatever houses I enter, I will go into them for the benefit of the sick, and will abstain from every voluntary act of mischief and corruption; and, further from the seduction of females or males, of freemen and slaves.

Whatever, in connection with my professional practice or not, in connection with it, I see or hear, in the life of men, which ought not to be spoken of abroad, I will not divulge, as reckoning that all such should be kept secret.

While I continue to keep this Oath unviolated, may it be granted to me to enjoy life and the practice of the art, respected by all men, in all times!

But should I trespass and violate this Oath, may the reverse be my lot!

<u>*Tallulah Muir 6/21/2024*</u>
Signed Date

"I shall do no harm"

Hippocratic Oath 'I shall do no harm'

BOOK SUMMARY

Back Cover

'Lulu and the Shape-Shifting Healers' takes you on a joyful adventure through time travel and alternate realms. This unique story introduces you to the most ancient physicians, Hippocrates and Dr. Hahnemann, and tells an unforgettable tale about a young girl stepping into her power. Lulu, an aspiring healer, is visited by the shapeshifting, blessed healers, the Angels, Jesus, the Holy Mother, and the Queen of the Merpeople. Experience magical, heartwarming tales of healing from lost eras, and immerse yourself in page-turning excitement filled with plant spirits, fairies, and ancient folklore.

Books By Rhea:

Coloring Book- Lulu and the Shape-Shifting Healers (2024)

Lulu and the Shape-Shifting Healers, (2024)

The Forgotten Realm, Volume I

Our Forgotten Allies, What's your Frequency (2018)

Acknowledgments

My acknowledgments have been and will always be my heroes. These heroes are the two beautiful souls I have admired since their birth. They have helped me to feel supported, loved, and lifted when I am in their presence—my wonderful children. I am honored to call you my children and even more so to have you call me Mom. Thank you both for your love and your guidance; you are cherished and loved so deeply. Your unwavering support for my far-out ideas is deeply appreciated; thank you both for being YOU and letting your immense lights shine and fill this world with that light. I love you both so much.

I'll love you forever, I'll like you for always,

as long as I'm living, my baby you'll be.

And, to my 'Solid as a Rock" mother and memory of my beloved dad. Mom, thank you for allowing me to read these pages to you over and over again. Thank you for your helpful and creative guidance. You have taught me so much about being positive and refocusing my attention in a direction that is more of a benefit. In memory of my Dad, I know you have been guiding me from page one; I miss you daily; we all do. May you rest in peace forevermore. You taught me so much; my cherished characteristic is how to show up for the ones we love. Thank you to my most amazing parents. I am honored to call you Mom & Dad.

Blessed Be!

About the Author

Rhea Iris Rivers is a Certified Herbalist, Nutritionist, Energy Healer, and HHP. She is a lifelong student of the healing arts, including Homeopathy. Rhea has a special interest in Women's Health and the well-being of our younger generations. 'Lulu and the Shape-Shifting Healers' is her second book. Her ability to connect with the Earth Mother has inspired her to overcome vaginal cancer, Lyme disease and detoxify from a breast implant rupture. She is a proud mother of two beautiful beings and enjoys being out in nature, public speaking, and sharing the magic of the healing arts.

website: ourforgottenallies.com
email: hello@ourforgotten.com
Books: Our Forgotten Allies, What's your Frequency
On Amazon (2018)
Lulu and the Shape-Shifting Healers - On Amazon
The Forgotten Realm, Volume I (2024)
Lulu and the Shape-Shifting Healers, Coloring Book